Disney FAIRIES

Storybook
Collection

THIS BOOK BELONGS TO

....

This edition published by Parragon Books Ltd in 2014

Parragon Books Ltd
Chartist House
15–17 Trim Street
Bath BA1 1HA, UK
www.parragon.com

ISBN 978-1-4723-5908-7

Printed in China

Disney FAIRIES

Storybook
Collection

PaRragon

Bath • New York • Cologne • Melbourne • Delhi
Hong Kong • Shenzhen • Singapore • Amsterdam

CONTENTS

The fairies were buzzing with excitement.
It was the day before the Pixie Hollow Games – a
series of sports events in which fairy-talent groups
competed against each other.

Rosetta was in charge of decorating the arena.
Suddenly, she gasped. A new garden fairy, named
Chloe, was heading straight for her flowers. And she
was carrying a large rock! Rosetta stopped Chloe
from knocking over the flowers, but mud
splattered everywhere.

When Rosetta discovered that Chloe was training for the games, she took her to the Fairy Hall of Honour.

"Notice anything unusual?" Rosetta asked.

"No garden-fairy team has ever come close to winning."

But Chloe only smiled. She was certain she was just the fairy to change that.

The next day, the talent groups gathered in the arena.
The Pixie Hollow Games were about to begin! To Chloe's
surprise, Rosetta had been chosen to be her partner.
Rosetta didn't think they could win, but she wore a fancy
dress so at least she would look fashionable.

Two storm fairies, Rumble and Glimmer, grinned at
each other. They were going for their fifth straight win.

The first event was the Leapfrogging Race.
Rosetta thought the frogs were completely gross.

But Chloe and Rosetta made it to the next round!
Their friends couldn't believe it. Even though they were
in last place, it was further than any garden-fairy team
had ever reached before!

Day two began with Dragonfly Waterskiing. It was terrifying! But Chloe coached Rosetta on her form and the two fairies zoomed across the finish line. The garden fairies were no longer in last place!

Next was the Twig Spheres Race. Chloe stood on top of their ball and ran backwards to make it roll. Rosetta was inside, steering.

When the race was over, the garden fairies had come in second – right after Rumble and Glimmer! Rumble didn't like it that the garden fairies were catching up.

Mouse Polo was the next event. Rosetta grinned as she passed the ball to Chloe, then charged up the field.

Chloe passed the ball back to her. Rosetta took a deep breath, aimed and scored! They had won another round!

The last event of the day was the Obstacle Course. The garden fairies hopped into flying teacups and took the lead. But the final obstacle was a slimy slug slide!

Rosetta refused to go down. As she and Chloe argued, everyone slid past them. They finally finished – last.

"Maybe we're just not cut out for this after all," said Chloe, defeated.

Rosetta felt terrible about making them lose the Obstacle Course. As she left the arena, she ran smack into Rumble.

"You keep getting in my way, don't you?" he said angrily. "Why don't you just stick to being pretty? That's what you're good at!"

Rosetta was furious. Somebody had to put Rumble in his place. She would prove him wrong!

The next day was the final event – the Pixie Cart Derby. When Rosetta arrived, the crowd gasped. She was dressed to compete! "I have a plan to win this whole thing," she told Chloe. "Just trust me, okay?"

Each team had built a special cart to drive in the derby. They all got off to a good start, but soon, only the storm fairies and the garden fairies were left in the race!

Mudslide Mountain loomed ahead. "This is our last chance to pass!" cried Chloe, looking at the shortcut.

"Now!" cried Rosetta. Since the fairies had been allowed to design their carts any way they liked, Rosetta had asked Tinker Bell to install a special lever on theirs. When she and Chloe pulled it, pinecones sprang out of the wheels to help them climb the mountain.

And once they reached the top, their cart turned into a giant sledge! Mud sprayed everywhere as they slid down the mountain, but Rosetta didn't care. Her plan was working. They zoomed right round Rumble and Glimmer!

But Rumble refused to be beaten.
He grabbed Glimmer's hand and
shot a bolt of lightning at Rosetta
and Chloe's cart.

KA-BOOM! The garden fairies'
cart flipped over.

Rosetta and Chloe knew they
couldn't win now, but they
began to push their
ruined cart. They were
determined to finish the
race, no matter what.

Rosetta and Chloe limped across the finish line.

"The winners," Queen Clarion announced, "are the garden fairies!"

"But I crossed the finish line first!" cried Rumble.

"Teammates must finish together," the queen reminded him.

Rumble turned and saw Glimmer on the other side of the finish line.

"Do you have any idea what you've done?" he cried.

"I helped the best team win," said Glimmer.

The crowd cheered as Queen Clarion smiled proudly at
the two garden fairies. Rosetta and Chloe couldn't believe it.

They had won the Pixie Hollow Games!

One winter's day in London,
a baby laughed for the very first
time. That laugh floated up and away
to meet its destiny. It would become
a fairy, just like all first laughs.

It flew straight for the Second Star
to the right, and passed through it
in a burst of light. On the other side
was ... Never Land!

The laugh floated towards a magical place in the heart of the island. This was Pixie Hollow, home of the fairies!

Vidia, the fastest-flying fairy of them all, guided the arrival into the Pixie Dust Tree. There, a dust-keeper named Terence sprinkled it with pixie dust, and it took the shape of a tiny, adorable fairy.

Clarion, queen of the fairies, helped the newcomer unfurl her two gossamer wings. The new fairy flapped her wings and realized she could fly!

Queen Clarion waved her hand and several toadstools sprung up around the Pixie Dust Well. Fairies immediately fluttered forwards to place different objects on these pedestals. "They will help you find your talent," the queen explained to the new fairy.

The youngster timidly placed her hand on a beautiful flower. Its glow instantly grew dim. She reached for a water droplet, but that, too, faded.

The fairy moved on without touching anything else – she was afraid to fail again – but then something amazing happened. As she passed by a hammer, it began to shine. Then it rose up off its pedestal and flew straight for her!

"I've never seen one glow that much before," said Silvermist.

Vidia glowered. She had one of the strongest and rarest talents in Pixie Hollow and she wasn't looking for competition.

"Tinker fairies," called the queen. "Welcome the newest member of your talent guild – Tinker Bell!"

Two tinker fairies, Clank and Bobble, whisked her off for a flying tour of Pixie Hollow. When the trio landed at Tinkers' Nook, Tink looked around and saw fairies fixing and fashioning all kinds of amazing, useful objects.

Next Clank and Bobble took Tinker Bell to her own little house, which had a wardrobe filled with clothes. Tinker Bell put on her new dress and tied her hair up. Then she reported to the workshop.

Soon Fairy Mary – the no-nonsense fairy who ran Tinkers' Nook – arrived. She noticed the new fairy's dainty hands. "Don't worry, dear, we'll build up those tinker muscles in no time," she exclaimed.

A little while later, Tink, Clank and Bobble were on their way to make deliveries. The friends heard a sound behind them. "Sprinting Thistles! *Aaaaagh!*" screamed Clank. The weeds nearby had come to life and were heading straight for them! The wagon lurched down the path and landed in a flowerbed in Springtime Square.

Rosetta, Silvermist, Iridessa and Fawn rushed over to help their friends. The tinkers were unhurt and soon ready to go back to their deliveries. They took some rainbow tubes to Iridessa. She explained that she would roll up rainbows, put them in the tubes and take them to the Mainland.

"What's the Mainland?" Tink asked.

"It's where we're going to go for spring, to change the seasons," replied Silvermist.

Next the tinkers stopped at the Flower Meadow, where Vidia was vacuuming the pollen out of flowers with her whirlwind.

"Hi! What's your talent?" Tink asked.

"I am a fast-flying fairy," answered Vidia. She made it clear that she didn't think much of tinker fairies.

"When I go to the Mainland, I'll prove just how important we are!" Tink replied.

Tink flew off, grumbling to herself. Soon, however, something down on the beach caught her attention. When she landed, she discovered several wonderful treasures buried in the sand.

"Lost Things," said Clank when Tink brought her finds to the Tinkers' Nook workshop.

"They wash up on Never Land from time to time," explained Bobble.

Fairy Mary whisked the trinkets away. The queen's review of the springtime preparations was that night and there was a lot to do.

Tink decided this was her chance to prove to Vidia just how important a tinker's talent really was!

That evening, the Minister of Spring welcomed Queen Clarion to the review ceremony.

"I think you'll find we have things well in hand," he said proudly. "When the Everblossom blooms, we will be ready to bring spring to the Mainland."

Suddenly, Tinker Bell interrupted the proceedings. "I came up with some fantastic things for tinkers to use when we go to the Mainland!" she told the queen excitedly.

"Has no one explained?" Queen Clarion said gently. "Tinker fairies don't go to the Mainland. All of those things are done by the nature-talent fairies. I'm sorry."

The next morning, Tink asked her friends to teach her how to be a nature fairy. She really wanted to go to the Mainland. Reluctantly, the other fairies agreed to help. No fairy had ever changed his or her talent before!

Tink's first lesson was on how to become a water fairy. Silvermist showed her how to place a dewdrop on a spider's web, but each time Tink tried, the dewdrop burst.

The light-fairy lesson didn't go any better. Tink lost control of the light and attracted a group of fireflies. They thought Tink's glow was irresistible!

Fawn had Tink's animal fairy lesson all planned.
"We're teaching baby birds how to fly," she announced.
Fawn went to a nest, smiled at a bird and gently encouraged it
until the fluffy little creature was flying along right behind her.
Unfortunately, Tink's baby bird seemed terrified. When she
nudged it towards the edge of the nest, it even tried to fight her!
"If I end up making acorn kettles the rest of my life,
I am holding you personally responsible," Tinker Bell
said impatiently to the bird.

Tink saw a majestic bird soaring in the sky and she decided to ask it to help her.

An ear-splitting screech filled the forest. The bird was a hawk!

Tink hurtled down into the knothole of a tree – but Vidia was already hiding there.

Tink accidentally slammed into Vidia and shot her out of the tree.

The hawk opened its beak, ready to strike. But luckily, the other fairies were able to chase the bird off.

Vidia was furious. Tink felt awful.

A little while later, Tinker Bell sat on the beach. She angrily threw a pebble and heard a *CLUNK!* Tink went to investigate and found a broken porcelain box.

By the time her friends found her, Tinker Bell was busily putting her discovery back together. The final touch was a lovely porcelain ballerina that fitted into the lid.

"Do you even realize what you're doing?" asked Rosetta. "Fixing stuff like this – that's what tinkering is!"

Tink realized that her friends didn't want her to change talents. Desperate, she went to visit the only fairy she thought might be able to help.

But Vidia was not in the mood for visitors – *especially* Tinker Bell.

"You're my last hope," pleaded Tink. "Rosetta won't even try to teach me to be a garden fairy now."

That gave Vidia an idea. She suggested that Tinker Bell prove she was a garden fairy by capturing the Sprinting Thistles.

Tink knew this was her last chance to go to the Mainland. She built a corral and made a lasso. She rode Cheese into Needlepoint Meadow and used twigs to herd a pair of Thistles into the corral.

"It's working!" Tink cried joyfully. But as she headed back out into the meadow, Vidia quietly blew open the corral gate. The two Thistles ran right out.

Soon other Thistles joined the two that had escaped. It was a stampede!
"Wait! Come back!" yelled Tinker Bell, riding after them.
The Thistles headed to Springtime Square, where they trampled over the carefully organized springtime supplies.
Just then, Queen Clarion appeared, a look of shock crossing her face. "By the Second Star ... all the preparations for spring!"
"I'm sorry," Tink whispered as she took to the sky.

Tink decided to leave Pixie Hollow forever, but she couldn't go without one last visit to the workshop. She had to admit that she *did* love to tinker.

At the workshop, she noticed Cheese sniffing around something at the back of the room — it was trinkets Fairy Mary had taken from her on her first day in Pixie Hollow.

"Lost Things ... that's it!" she cried as she took them over to her worktable. Tink thought she had an idea that would fix everything.

That night, Queen Clarion gathered all the fairies and explained that spring would not come that year. There simply wasn't enough time to replace all the supplies that had been ruined.

"Wait!" Tinker Bell cried. "I know how we can fix everything!" The clever fairy had designed speedy machines to mend what the Thistles had trampled. She had even used Lost Things to repair her paint sprayer.

Tink showed a group of fairies how to assemble a machine to make berry paint. Next she rigged up a vacuum that could collect huge amounts of seeds at a time.

The fairies worked all night using Tink's machines. Early the next morning, Queen Clarion and the ministers of the seasons flew into the square. Before them were more spring supplies than they had ever seen!

The sun rose, and the Everblossom opened and gave off a golden glow, signalling that it was time to bring springtime to the world. The fairies cheered.

"You did it, Tinker Bell," congratulated Queen Clarion.

"We *all* did it," Tink replied.

Tink was allowed to go to the Mainland to return the music box she had fixed.

Tinker Bell found the home where the music box belonged and tapped on the window. A little girl poked her head out of the window. Her face was filled with joy at the discovery of her long-lost treasure.

Soon the fairies' work was done and they had to return to Never Land. Tink couldn't wait to go home – she had tinkering to do!

In Pixie Hollow, Terence and the other dust-keeper fairies were bagging and delivering pixie dust from the Pixie Dust Tree. It was pixie dust that made it possible for all fairies to do their special kinds of magic. As usual, when the day's work was done, Terence headed off to help his best friend Tinker Bell with her latest invention.

When Terence found Tink, she was preparing to take a boat she had just built for a test run. The Pixie Dust Express seemed to be working perfectly – until it ran into a tree.

"I can't believe the boat broke!" Tinker Bell exclaimed to Terence.

"Ah, it just needs a little tinkering," Terence said breezily. He always knew how to make Tink feel better.

Suddenly, a fairy named Viola interrupted them to announce that Queen Clarion wanted to see Tinker Bell right away!

Tink nervously went to the royal chambers, where Queen Clarion, the Minister of Autumn and Fairy Mary were waiting for her.

The minister explained that this year's celebration of the end of autumn – the Autumn Revelry – coincided with a blue harvest moon. A new sceptre had to be created for the occasion and Fairy Mary had recommended Tinker Bell.

Tink couldn't believe it!

"At the top of the sceptre you will place a moonstone," the minister explained. "When the blue moon is at its peak, its rays will pass through the gem, creating Blue Pixie Dust. The Blue Pixie Dust restores the Pixie Dust Tree."

The group made their way to the ornate case that held the moonstone, but Tinker Bell bumped into the case.

"It has been handed down from generation to generation," said Fairy Mary. "It is ridiculously fragile. You have to be careful!"

Tink was touched to be given such an honour. She reverently took the case holding the moonstone, bowed and left the chamber.

For the next few days, Tink tried out different designs for the sceptre. Her friend Terence was always there to help.

As time wore on, though, Tink began to find Terence a bit less helpful. He made too much noise. He got in her way. He sometimes stoked the fire so much that the room filled with smoke. Still, she tried to be patient. He meant well.

Finally, the day came for Tink to place the moonstone on top of the sceptre. Terence hovered over her, offering a steady stream of advice.

"Will you please...." begged Tink through clenched teeth. Then a piece of the setting broke and Terence went off to find Tink a sharp tool to fix it.

He proudly returned with a compass, but Tink was annoyed. The compass was the exact opposite of sharp! She bumped it aside and the compass fell on the sceptre. Her creation was ruined!

Tink exploded in anger. "Out!" she ordered. "You brought this stupid thing here. This is your fault."

"Fine! Last time I try to help you!" Terence yelled back.

Tink placed the moonstone on a cushion and began to pace. In frustration, she kicked the compass with all her might.

The cover popped open – and crushed the moonstone!

"No!" Tinker Bell gasped in horrror.

Tinker Bell went to Fairy Mary, who was waiting for a show to
start at the fairy-tale theatre. Tink tried to work up the courage to
admit she had broken the moonstone, but she just couldn't do it.
Fairy Mary was counting on her!

Then the show began, and a storytelling fairy named Lyria
appeared on the stage. She told of a day long ago when pirates
arrived in Never Land and captured a fairy. The pirates had forced
her to lead them to the enchanted Mirror of Incanta, which had the
power to grant three wishes. The pirates had made two wishes, but
then their ship was wrecked and the mirror had been lost forever.

Tink listened closely and learned that the pirates' ship remained on an island north of Never Land. It could be found by following the way marked by a stone arch and an old bridge. Legend had it that the mirror still lay somewhere deep within the wreck.

Pretending to be tired, Tink left the theatre as quickly as she could. She had to find that mirror and wish to restore the moonstone!

Back at home, Tink drew a map, consulted her compass and gathered together some supplies. Then she set about building a balloon that could carry her and everything she needed to the lost island. When it was finished, she sprinkled the balloon with pixie dust and lifted off with the moonstone fragments safely tucked in her satchel.

As night fell, Tinker Bell looked into her supply bag for a snack. Her food was gone – and in its place was a very full firefly!

She shooed the bug away, then turned her attention to the map – but it was too dark to see. The firefly, named Blaze, was there to help.

"You can stay," Tink said, giving in. "For now."

The balloon flew into a cloud bank and eventually came to rest in a tree. When the clouds cleared, Tink could see they were on an island!

Excited, she left Blaze in charge of the balloon and went off to investigate. But as soon as Tink had left, the balloon came loose and started to drift away. By the time Blaze caught Tink's attention, it had gone!

Tink and Blaze set off to find the balloon, but by now Tinker Bell was out of pixie dust and could no longer fly.

Soon the pair found the stone arch and then, a little while later, the old bridge. Tink had thought the story's instructions warned her about a "toll" bridge, but she quickly realized it was really a "troll" bridge! Luckily, the troll guards were so busy squabbling that they didn't even notice when Tink and Blaze sneaked past them.

Tink and Blaze continued to the island. Finally, they could see the pirates' shipwreck! Tink and Blaze ventured into the damp, cold ship, even though it made them shiver with fright.

"Look, Blaze," said Tink. There, illuminated by a shaft of light, was a satchel.

Tinker Bell hurled the compass needle at the bag and – RIIIP! – lost fairy treasure spilled out into a heap on the floor.

Tink reached into the treasure, rooted around and pulled out the mirror! She laid the fragments of the moonstone in front of it and prepared to make her wish. But every time she tried, Blaze distracted her by buzzing near her ear.

"Blaze, I wish you'd be quiet for one minute!" Tinker Bell said sternly.

Suddenly, the buzzing stopped.

"No, that one didn't count!" Tinker Bell wailed. She'd lost her one chance to fix the moonstone!

Terence's face appeared in the mirror.

"Terence!" Tink exclaimed. She missed her friend terribly. "I am so sorry."

"I forgive you," replied Terence, "but why didn't you tell me about the moonstone?"

"I didn't think I needed any help," Tink explained. "I was wrong. I wish you were here."

But Terence was there!

He had gone to Tink's house and found bits of the shattered moonstone as well as the diagram of her balloon. He guessed Tinker Bell needed help and had flown until he had found her. He had even discovered her balloon! Tink was overjoyed to see him.

Terence led Tink and Blaze back to the balloon. Luckily, Tink had just enough pixie dust in one of the bags inside to get the balloon back into the air.

"I don't know if it will help, but I brought this," said Terence. He handed Tink the shattered sceptre.

"Hey, I've got an idea," Tink announced to Terence. "Would you help me?"

Together, they worked through the night to repair the broken sceptre as the blue moon rose in the sky.

The Autumn Revelry was already underway when Tink,
Terence and Blaze arrived back in Pixie Hollow.

Tink knelt before the queen and unveiled the sceptre. It was
fashioned from the broken bits of the sceptre, the bent mirror
frame and fragments of the moonstone.

"Please work," Tinker Bell whispered as the rays from the blue
moon began to touch the sceptre.

WHOOSH! The moonbeams reflected everywhere and rained
down rare Blue Pixie Dust.

At first a flurry, then a blizzard, the dust swirled in the air before settling in drifts on the ground.

"Your Majesty!" the Minister of Autumn cried jubilantly. "I've never seen this much Blue Pixie Dust before!"

Fairy Mary agreed. "It's at least a million smidges. Maybe more."

Silvermist, Fawn, Iridessa and Rosetta were amazed. "Only Tinker Bell," Iridessa said affectionately.

"Tonight is our finest revelry ever," Queen Clarion said, "thanks to one very special fairy – Tinker Bell."

Tink let everyone know she couldn't have done it without her friends Terence and Blaze.

"To the Pixie Dust Tree," the Minister of Autumn announced as Tinker Bell led the procession.

And so that night passed into fairy legend.

Disney
FAIRIES

TinkerBell
and the
SECRET
of the
WINGS

The Winter Woods was the most mysterious place in Pixie Hollow – full of shimmering snowflakes and glistening icicles.

Queen Clarion had made a rule that warm-season fairies weren't allowed to go there. But, one day, curious Tinker Bell jumped across the border! When she landed on the other side, her wings sparkled strangely....

Back at
home, Tink
wanted to know
what had caused
her wings to sparkle.
She wrapped up in her warmest
coat for a trip back to the Winter
Woods. She hid inside a snowflake
basket that was being flown there by an owl.

When she had landed safely in the Winter Woods,
Tink went to the Hall of Winter to find the Keeper
of All Fairy Knowledge, Dewey.
Tink was amazed when she saw him talking to
a winter fairy whose wings were glowing brightly!

Suddenly, Tink's wings
began to sparkle again!
Tinker Bell and the winter fairy,
Periwinkle, looked at each other's
glittering wings in amazement.

Dewey explained that Tink and Peri had been born
of the same laugh – which meant that they were sisters!
The girls couldn't believe it!

"That is why your wings sparkle," Dewey told them.

89

Tink should have gone straight home to the warm seasons, but Dewey said that she and Peri could spend a little time together first.

So, Peri gave Tink a tour of the Winter Woods. They went for an exciting ride down a frozen waterfall with Peri's friends, Gliss and Spike.

After dark, the Winter Woods got even colder,
so Tink built a fire to keep warm. She told Peri
all about her home.

"I wish I could go there," Peri said. "But I can't live
in warm weather."

"I made it warmer over here ... " replied Tinker Bell.
"Maybe I could make it colder over there."

Just then, the snow floor crumbled beneath them.
The fire was melting it!

A snowy lynx picked up Tink and Peri and took them
back to Dewey, who told Tink that she must return home.

Tinker Bell had an idea. She hugged Peri and whispered,
"Meet me back here tomorrow!"

When Tink arrived back home, she told her friends all about Periwinkle. She also shared her idea with them – a snowmaker! They got straight to work building the machine, which would make it cold enough for Peri to visit Tink.

The next day, they brought the snowmaker to the border. "This is your ticket to the warm side of Pixie Hollow!" Tink told Peri and her friends.

Lord Milori – the Lord of Winter – was waiting for them at the edge of the Winter Woods.

"This is why we do not cross the border," he said. "The rule is there to protect you."

At that moment, Queen Clarion, the queen of Pixie Hollow, arrived. She agreed that the rule was for everyone's safety.

Lord Milori pushed the snowmaker into the icy river as Tink and Peri unhappily hugged goodbye.

Back at home, Queen Clarion tried to help Tinker Bell to understand the rule. She told Tink about a warm-season fairy and a winter fairy who had fallen in love a long time ago. One of the fairies had broken a wing because they had crossed the border – and there was no cure for a broken wing.

As Queen Clarion spoke, Tink looked out of the window and saw something strange – snowflakes were falling!

At the border of the Winter Woods, the snowmaker was stuck at the top of a waterfall. Chunks of ice from the river were pouring into it and it was spraying out snow!

The fairies managed to push the snowmaker out of the waterfall, but it was too late – the seasons had been thrown out of balance.

Everyone was worried – a freeze was now on its way to the warm part of Pixie Hollow. If the Pixie Dust Tree froze, there would be no more pixie dust!

The fairies got straight to work. Some rounded up insects to bring them to shelter ...

... while others rushed to cover the tree with blankets of moss. Would they be able to save it?

Then, Tink remembered the flower that Peri had coated with frost. She flew to the Winter Woods to find her sister.

"I think there's something you can do!" Tink said urgently. "Your frost – it kept the flower alive."

Gliss explained that frost was like a little blanket. It tucked warm air inside – keeping out the cold.

"We could frost the Pixie Dust Tree!" Peri realized.

The winter fairies worked together to quickly frost the Pixie Dust Tree before the freeze hit. After the freeze had passed, the sun came out and melted the ice from the tree. Slowly, the pixie dust started flowing again. The tree was saved!

But Tink realized that she had broken a wing when she had flown back to the Winter Woods. As the sisters said goodbye, an explosion of light burst from their wings. The magic between them healed Tink's wing!

From that day on, warm-season fairies could visit the winter fairies whenever they liked! All they needed was a little frost to keep their wings safe. Tink and Peri would never have to say goodbye again.

106

Tinker Bell and her fairy friends from Pixie Hollow
were on their way to bring summer to the Mainland!

Summer needed the fairies' constant attention – which
meant that Tink was going to be on the Mainland for
months instead of days. She was very excited!

Tink and her friend Terence, a dust-keeper fairy, landed in a clearing.

Tinker Bell looked around the peaceful meadow. "Where is everyone?"

"Tink," said Terence, "fairy camp is in here." He walked over to a huge oak tree and pulled back a thick tangle of leaves.

"Wow!" cried Tink. Hidden beneath the tree, an entire fairy community bustled with activity.

Just then, a loud CRACK! went through the fairy camp! Fawn knocked over some paint that fairies were using to decorate butterfly wings and the splattered butterfly took off.

The other fairies hid, but Tinker Bell had to see what had made the noise. Vidia chased after her, trying to get her to come back. Tink ignored her and flew down to discover some humans and their car. Tink waited for the humans to go in their house before examining the car .

Tinker Bell darted inside the engine. She found an interesting-looking lever and turned it over and over again. Outside the car, each turn of the lever showered Vidia with water!

Tink flew back out and looked Vidia up and down. "You're all wet," she remarked.

Just then, the door to the house opened and out walked Lizzy and her father, Dr Griffiths.

The humans' attention was focused on a butterfly.

"The wings have two entirely different patterns," Dr Griffiths observed.

"Well, I guess that's just the way the fairies decided to paint it," Lizzy said.

"Fairies do not paint butterfly wings, because as you know, *fairies are not real*," her father declared.

If Vidia hadn't stopped her, Tinker Bell would have flown out and proven that fairies existed right then and there!

Meanwhile, Lizzy was playing with a small house she had built. "Would you like to help me with it?" she asked her father.

"I'm sorry, dear," Dr Griffiths said. "I have to present my exhibit to the museum tomorrow. Now run along...."

Tink and Vidia were exploring. "Wow!" exclaimed Tink. She landed next to a row of buttons lined up like stepping stones. "These will be perfect for the new wagon prototype I've been working on."

"I'm not carrying this human junk back to camp...." began Vidia, but then she spotted something that made her stop in her tracks. It was Lizzy's fairy house.

Vidia wanted to leave, but Tinker Bell headed straight for the house!

Tink went inside the house, ignoring Vidia's warnings that humans could be dangerous. Frustrated, Vidia whipped up a gust of wind that slammed the door shut.

Tink didn't mind. She was having fun exploring the tiny house's gadgets.

Suddenly, Vidia saw a human approaching in the distance. She pulled on the door to let Tink out, but it was jammed!

Lizzy went to pick up her fairy house, and was amazed to see a tiny fairy inside. Finally, she had proof that fairies were real! She ran back to her home, while Tinker Bell bounced around inside the fairy house.

The little girl went upstairs to her room, and peeked in the fairy house. But Tinker Bell was nowhere to be seen.

"Where have you gone?" wondered Lizzy. She took the roof off the house and *ZIP!* Tink darted out.

Mr Twitches, the family cat, immediately lunged for the fairy.

As a horrified Vidia watched at the window, Lizzy put Tinker Bell in a birdcage for safekeeping.

Vidia knew she had to free Tinker Bell, but she couldn't do it alone. She flew back to the fairy camp to get help.

She explained to her friends what had happened – but a storm had just erupted.

"We can't fly in the rain," Fawn reminded her. "And the meadow's already flooded!"

Clank and Bobble had a plan. They would build a boat!

Back at the house, Lizzy let Tinker Bell out of the cage.

"You don't have to be scared," said Lizzy. "I'm very nice. Look, I've been drawing fairies all my life."

Tinker Bell was amazed by Lizzy's fairy collection. But as Lizzy described what was going on in each picture, Tink realized the little girl had her fairy facts all wrong!

Tinker Bell pointed to the window.

"You want to go?" asked Lizzy. "I understand." She went to the window and opened it wide.

Tink made it as far as the windowsill and stopped. It was pouring outside!

"Can't you fly in the rain?" guessed Lizzy. "You can stay with me until it stops. That way you can teach me more about fairies!"

Back on the fairy boat, the rescuers were in a panic. They were heading straight for a waterfall!

Thinking quickly, Vidia hovered in front of the boat and created a burst of wind. The boat started to turn round!

But, several large raindrops soaked Vidia's wings and she had to stop. The boat was swept towards the falls again.

"Hang on, we're going straight down!" yelled Bobble.

At the last second, Silvermist made water rise up so that the drop wasn't as steep. The boat crashed onshore, but the fairies were all right!

"I guess our sailing days are over," said Bobble.

Back at the house, Tink and Lizzy created a Fairy Field Guide, filled with information about the world of fairies.

By the time they were done, the rain was easing up. Tinker Bell and Lizzy both realized it was time for Tink to go home. As much as she was going to miss the little girl, Tink was really excited to get back to her fairy friends.

But as Tinker Bell flew away from Lizzy's house, she saw the little girl trying to show her father the Fairy Field Guide. Dr Griffiths was too busy trying to fix the leaks in their home to listen to Lizzy. Tinker Bell watched Lizzy walk sadly away from her father. Tink realized she had to find a way to bring father and daughter together and make them happy again.

Lizzy thought Tink had left, but to Lizzy's surprise Tinker Bell suddenly appeared. The look of joy on Lizzy's face let Tink know that coming back had been the right thing to do.

Lizzy went to sleep, and Tinker Bell watched as Dr Griffiths came up to check on her. "There just aren't enough hours in the day," he said to his daughter. It warmed Tink's heart and she felt even better about finding a way to help them.

Meanwhile, the other fairies were continuing their mission to find Tink on foot. Vidia spotted the muddy road that led to Lizzy's house. Vidia helped her friends across, but then got stuck in the mud herself. Silvermist, Fawn, Rosetta and Iridessa grabbed on to her and pulled, but she wouldn't budge.

The fairies saw a car coming towards them, but Iridessa was able to save them by reflecting the light from the car. The driver got out of his car. "Hello? Is somebody out there?" he asked.

Fawn grabbed his shoelace and instructed the others to hold on tight. When the driver turned to leave, they were all pulled out of the mud!

Back at the house, Tinker Bell had secretly fixed all the leaks in the house for Dr Griffiths. Before she returned to Lizzy's room, she couldn't help but notice the butterfly fluttering in a jar on Dr Griffiths's desk. It made Tink feel terrible.

The next day, Lizzy went to her father's office. She could see that Dr Griffiths was upset about something.

"The butterfly is gone," he announced. "There is no one else in this house, there's only one logical explanation. It must have been you."

"It wasn't," replied Lizzy. "I could tell you who did it, but you wouldn't believe me."

"Very well," Dr Griffiths said. "Off to your room. I'm very disappointed with you."

Back in Lizzy's room, Tinker Bell was apologizing for getting
the little girl into trouble.

"I'm glad you're here," Lizzy told Tink. "You're my best friend.
I wish I were a fairy just like you. Then I could fly around with
the other fairies all the time."

That gave Tinker Bell an idea! She instructed Lizzy to close
her eyes and spread out her arms. Then the fairy hovered above
Lizzy's head and showered it with pixie dust.

Just then, the other fairies entered the house.

"Okay," began Vidia. "Tinker Bell is upstairs. The little girl has her in a cage."

"Great!" Fawn exclaimed. "Anything else?"

But before Vidia could reply, Fawn had her answer. Mr Twitches was standing in the doorway!

Meanwhile, Dr Griffiths heard noises coming from upstairs. "What's going on in here?" Dr Griffiths demanded as he entered Lizzy's room.

Lizzy had to hold on to the furniture to stop herself from floating off the floor. "I was flying," she said. "My fairy showed me how."

While the other fairies distracted Mr Twitches, Vidia headed to save Tinker Bell. Vidia got there just as Tink revealed herself to Dr Griffiths. He tried to catch Tink, but Vidia pushed her out of the way! Dr Griffiths ran out of the house with Vidia instead. "I must get this to the museum right away!" declared Dr Griffiths as he dashed down the stairs.

The other fairies had tamed Mr Twitches with some catnip that Rosetta and Fawn had found. They rode on the now friendly cat and entered Lizzy's room. Tinker Bell and Lizzy were trying to figure out how to get Dr Griffiths to release Vidia.

"We can't fly in this weather," said Tink, "but I think I know somebody who can."

The fairies swirled round Lizzy and showered her with pixie dust.

"All aboard!" cried Tinker Bell.

Lizzy had a rough start, but was soon flying smoothly above the country road that led to the city.

A little while later, the magnificent sight of London came into view.

Once they got closer, Tinker Bell flew into Dr Griffiths's car's engine and brought the car to a stop.

"Father!" Lizzy called. Dr Griffiths turned to see his daughter flying towards him, pixie dust trailing behind her.

Dr Griffiths couldn't believe his eyes! "How are you doing that?" he asked. "There's no feasible scientific explanation. It has to be ... magic."

Lizzy told her father that they had to take the fairies back to the country. Seeing Tink and the other fairies, her father understood. Seconds later, Vidia was reunited with her friends.

Dr Griffiths and Lizzy waved goodbye to their new friends as the fairies headed back to work.

One beautiful day in Pixie Hollow, Rosetta, Silvermist and
Iridessa were planting sunflowers when Zarina walked past.
"Hey, Zarina! Out of pixie dust again?" asked Rosetta.
Fairies use pixie dust to fly, but Zarina preferred to walk.
"Just out for a stroll. You know me!" Zarina said.

Zarina was a dust-keeper fairy and, one day, it was her turn to pour the special Blue Pixie Dust into the Pixie Dust Tree.

The Blue Pixie Dust was powerful – mixing it with golden pixie dust made the gold dust multiply!

Zarina asked Fairy Gary, the head dust-keeper, if they could make other colours of pixie dust. Fairy Gary warned her, "Dust-keepers are forbidden to tamper with pixie dust."

Zarina had secretly been saving up her pixie dust.
After finding a speck of Blue Dust in her hair, Zarina
was inspired to try one of her many failed pixie-dust
experiments again, this time adding a tiny bit of the
Blue Dust speck.

The gold dust turned orange!

Zarina shared her discovery
with her friend Tinker Bell –
the new orange dust allowed
Zarina to bend
a moonbeam!

Zarina wanted to experiment more! But Tink was concerned. "Zarina, I really think you should stop," she said firmly.

Zarina turned and accidentally bumped into a plant, spilling all of her new pink dust on it. The plant's vines grew quickly, bursting out of Zarina's cottage and spreading all over Pixie Hollow. They even crushed the Dust Depot.

Zarina couldn't believe the damage!

When Fairy Gary saw the pink dust, he knew Zarina had been experimenting with pixie dust. He told Zarina she could no longer be a dust-keeper fairy. "You were told not to tamper with pixie dust."

She was devastated. She rushed back home, packed her things and left Pixie Hollow.

One year later, the fairies were celebrating the Four Seasons Festival.

While Periwinkle dazzled the crowd at the amphitheatre with her ice-skating skills, Tink and her friends were backstage working on their act for the show.

As everyone watched Periwinkle's performance, Tinker Bell saw a fairy sprinkling pink dust behind the crowd.

"Wait. Is that ... Zarina?" asked Tink.

Suddenly, flowers
sprouted in the
amphitheatre – and then
they burst open and sprayed
pollen into the air. Rosetta knew
it would make everyone fall asleep.
"Guys! We gotta hide – now!"

After Tink and her friends came out of hiding, they discovered the Blue Pixie Dust was missing!

They followed its blue glow to a rowing boat where they saw Zarina showing the bag of Blue Dust to pirates! Tinker Bell assumed that the pirates had made Zarina take the dust.

But then the fairies watched in shock as a pirate called James said to Zarina, "Let me say, your plan worked perfectly ... *captain*."

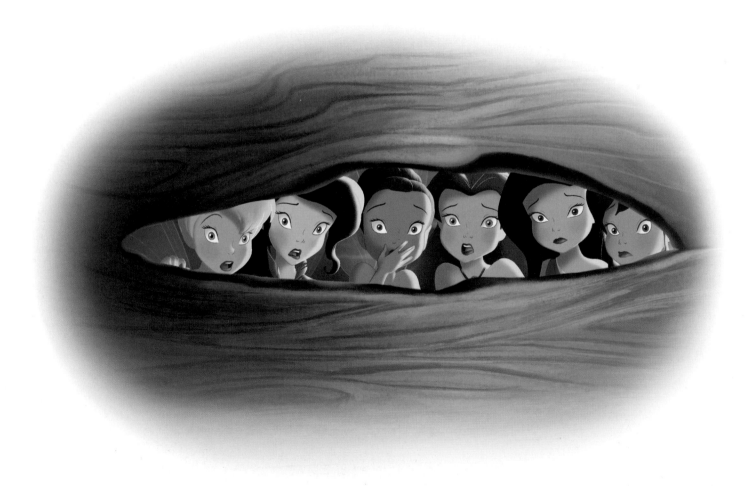

The fairies snatched the bag of
Blue Pixie Dust from the pirates
and flew away from the boat.

"Give me back that dust!"
shouted Zarina as she
chased after them.

Zarina threw multicoloured dust at the fairies, knocking them through a waterfall and out cold. Zarina took back the bag of Blue Pixie Dust and flew off.

When the fairies woke up they discovered that the dust had swapped their talents – and their outfits!

The fairies found the pirate ship that the rowing boat had been taking the Blue Pixie Dust to and they sneaked aboard.

The ship sailed to Skull Rock where, inside, Zarina had grown a Pixie Dust Tree. The pirates wanted the pixie dust from the tree to make their ship fly! Some of the fairies sneaked into Zarina's cabin, where they listened to James and Zarina's plans. The others tried to listen from outside.

James watched Zarina preparing the Blue Pixie Dust. "So the secret is to put the Blue Dust directly into the tree. Very impressive, captain!"

Inside Skull Rock, Zarina and James made their way to the tree. Slowly, Zarina tipped a container of Blue Dust into the dust well of the tree. Then she saw the fairies.

Zarina drew her sword and called to her pirate friends, who caught the fairies in nets.

"Zarina, don't do this! Come back home," begged Tinker Bell.

"I'll never go back to Pixie Hollow," answered Zarina. "This is exactly where I belong."

Tink and the others were taken to the galley, where the ship's cook put them in an old crab cage. The fairies tried their best to escape, but they were locked up tight.

Meanwhile, Zarina added Blue Pixie Dust to the tree, which started to make golden dust flow. The pirates cheered! Their plan had been a success.

Zarina sprinkled the golden dust on James. She taught him to fly and they soared through the air together. But when they landed back on the ship, James locked Zarina in a lantern. Now that he had the dust, he revealed he had been using her – he had never been her friend.

The fairies finally
managed to escape.
They did not want
Zarina to get hurt,
despite her actions.
They rushed to help
their misguided friend.

Zarina was grateful
to Tink and her friends.
She apologized and
offered to help them
catch James.

Zarina led the fairies to the flying ship and they slipped into the captain's cabin undetected – and reappeared looking like swashbucklers!

But the fairies struggled to fight the pirates with their tiny swords.

They realized that if they used their talents together they could defeat the pirates.

Fawn used her new light talent to shoot scorching light-beams down at the pirates.

While Zarina and James fought, the ship started to tip over. James clung to the mast trying not to fall in the sea.

Zarina grabbed the vial of Blue Pixie Dust that he had around his neck. When he saw the golden pixie dust start to fall from the ship into the sea he reached for it and fell!

As he fell, he was covered with the
golden dust. He then began to fly! He swiped
the blue dust back from Zarina. But one tiny speck
of Blue Dust fell from the vial and Zarina threw it at
James. That made the pixie dust multiply all over James and
he flew wildly – right into the ocean!

The fairies congratulated each other on defeating the pirates and turned the ship round.

Zarina, Tink and the other fairies flew the ship back to Pixie Hollow and Zarina used her dust to wake up everyone in the amphitheatre. Everyone was very happy that Zarina had come back home! The fairies returned the Blue Dust to the vault and Pixie Hollow was saved.

The End